A NOTE TO PARENTS

Reading Aloud with Your Child

Research shows that reading books alo[ud] valuable support parents can pr[ovide]a[s] children learn to read.

- Be a ham! The more enthusiasm you display, the more your child will enjoy the book.
- Run your finger underneath the words as you read to signal that the print carries the story.
- Leave time for examining the illustrations more closely; encourage your child to find things in the pictures.
- Invite your youngster to join in whenever there's a repeated phrase in the text.
- Link up events in the book with similar events in your child's life.
- If your child asks a question, stop and answer it. The book can be a means to learning more about your child's thoughts.

Listening to Your Child Read Aloud

The support of your attention and praise is absolutely crucial to your child's continuing efforts to learn to read.

- If your child is learning to read and asks for a word, give it immediately so that the meaning of the story is not interrupted. DO NOT ask your child to sound out the word.
- On the other hand, if your child initiates the act of sounding out, don't intervene.
- If your child is reading along and makes what is called a miscue, listen for the sense of the miscue. If the word "road" is substituted for the word "street," for instance, no meaning is lost. Don't stop the reading for a correction.
- If the miscue makes no sense (for example, "horse" for "house"), ask your child to reread the sentence because you're not sure you understand what's just been read.
- Above all else, enjoy your child's growing command of print and make sure you give lots of praise. *You are your child's first teacher — and the most important one. Praise from you is critical for further risk-taking and learning.*

—Priscilla Lynch
Ph.D, New York University
Educational Consultant

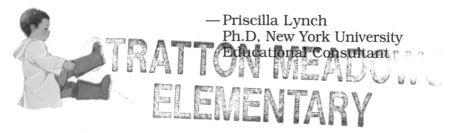

STRATTON MEADOWS
ELEMENTARY

To my sweet husband Michael, who was very good at
pouting and shouting as a child
—A.S.M.

To Wallace, my heart-and-soul mate
—S.W.

Text copyright © 1995 by Angela Shelf Medearis.
Illustrations copyright © 1995 by Sylvia Walker.
All rights reserved. Published by Scholastic Inc.
HELLO READER!, CARTWHEEL BOOKS, and the
CARTWHEEL BOOKS logo are registered trademarks of Scholastic Inc.

Library of Congress Cataloging-in-Publication Data

Medearis, Angela Shelf.
      We play on a rainy day / by Angela Shelf Medearis ; illustrated by
Sylvia Walker.
      p.   cm — (Hello reader! Level 1)
   Summary: Children pout when the rain begins, but, soon, properly dressed,
they enjoy playing outdoors in the rain.
   ISBN 0-590-26265-3
   [1. Rain and rainfall—Fiction.   2. Play—Fiction.   3. Stories in rhyme.]
I. Walker, Sylvia, ill.   II. Title.   III. Series: Hello reader! Level 1
PZ8.3.M551155We   1995
[E]—dc20
                                                            94-38221
                                                              CIP
                                                               AC
12 11 10 9 8 7 6 5 4   5 6 7 8 9/9 0/0

Printed in the U.S.A.   **24**

First Scholastic printing, May 1995

We Play on a Rainy Day

by Angela Shelf Medearis
Illustrated by Sylvia Walker

Hello Reader! — Level 1

SCHOLASTIC INC.
New York   Toronto   London   Auckland   Sydney

We skate.

We run.

We have fun
in the sun.

We ride.

We slide.

We swing.

We sing.

The clouds come
one by one.

Good-bye, sun.

It rains. It pours.

We run indoors.

We pout.
We shout.

"We want to go out!"
"We want to go out!"

We wear hats.
We wear coats.

We wear boots, too.
Purple, red, blue.

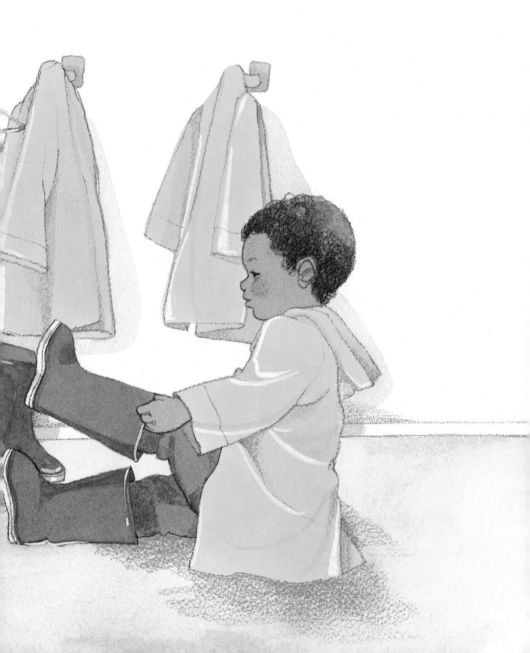

Boats float.

Mud pies bake.

We play in puddles
the rain makes.

We splash.

We play.

We have fun on a rainy day.